A MIGHTY BIG WISH

by
Kim Ostrow

illustrated by
Victoria Miller

SCHOLASTIC INC.

New York   Toronto   London   Auckland   Sydney
Mexico City   New Delhi   Hong Kong   Buenos Aires

Butch Hartman

Based on the TV series *The Fairly OddParents*®
created by Butch Hartman as seen on Nickelodeon®

ISBN 0-439-66668-6

12 11 10 9 8 7 6 5 4 3 2 1   4 5 6 7 8 9/0

Printed in the U.S.A.

First Scholastic printing, September 2004

It was Timmy Turner's
first day of school.
He adjusted his pink hat,
grabbed his backpack,
and walked out the door.

Timmy thought of the things
he loved about school.

His favorite activity was
eating lunch with his pals
and talking about really
serious subjects . . . like comics!

But then Timmy remembered
the worst part of school—
Francis the bully!

Timmy frowned.
"I do not want to spend
another year getting
pushed around by a big bully.
This year, Timmy Turner
is not going to take it!"

Timmy tried to make a muscle
to show Cosmo and Wanda
how strong he was.
"I wish I was bigger!"
said Timmy brightly.

POOF!

Timmy's wish came true.

He was huge!

"Awesome!" shouted Timmy.

"I am living large!"

"What did the giant boy say?"

Cosmo asked.

"Timmy is too far up. I can't hear a

thing!" said Wanda.

"Let's see Francis

bother me now!" said Timmy.

When Timmy got to school he had to

squeeze through the front door.

"Remember to duck!" Wanda

reminded him.

"And remember to goose!"

added Cosmo.

BONK!

"Ouch!" said Timmy.

"I guess that's just part of being big."

Timmy spotted Chester and
A.J. by their lockers.
"Hey, guys!" his voice boomed.
"What happened to you?"
Chester asked, confused.

"Oh . . . uh . . . I have been
lifting weights," said Timmy.
"Since yesterday?" asked A.J.
"It's impossible to grow that
much in one day."

"Not if you take powerful vitamins,"
said Timmy, thinking fast.
"Where did you get them?" A.J. asked.

"Internet," replied Timmy.

His friends gave him a funny look.

"Anyway, now I can protect us
from Francis," declared Timmy.

On the way to math
class Timmy stopped
at his locker to get his
book.

But his hands were
too big to fit inside!

Later Timmy went to the locker room
to change for gym class.
He barely fit into his clothes.
"Just act natural. Then no one
will notice that your clothes
are way too small," Cosmo said.

"This will all be worth it
when Francis sees me!"
Timmy reminded himself
as he wiggled into his clothes.

In gym there was no dodgeball game.

The kids were too scared

of Timmy's throws.

Instead, they did jumping jacks.

"Way to go, Turner. You're no fun!"

said his classmates.

In science no one could see
the blackboard over
Timmy's huge head.
He had to move to the back
of the class with the frogs.

At lunch Timmy broke the table when he put down his tray. Chester and A.J. stood behind him trying to catch the flying food!

Just when he was getting tired of
being huge, Timmy spotted Francis.
He puffed up his shoulders
and tried to look tough.
Francis walked through the cafeteria
pushing kids out of his way.

Timmy was so big that
Francis didn't even see him.
He thought Timmy was a pillar.
"Hey!" shouted Timmy.
"Look at me!" Francis looked
around, but he could not
figure out where the voice
was coming from.

Recess was no fun at all.

Timmy got stuck trying to

go down the slide.

Next, he tried the swings.

But that didn't work either.

"This plan is not working at all,"
said Timmy, pouting.
Timmy was fed up with being big.
He sat down right on top of
Cosmo and Wanda. Oops!

"Timmy does not know his own strength!" gasped Wanda. But Timmy did not notice. "This is the worst first day of school ever," said Timmy.

"No one played with me in gym.

I broke everything I touched.

And Francis did not even see me!

I wish I were small again."

Cosmo and Wanda heard Timmy's wish.

They tried to raise their wands

but they were trapped.

Timmy stood up.

Cosmo and Wanda were free.

"Boy, am I glad to see

you guys," said Timmy.

"I wish I was normal-size again!"

Cosmo and Wanda let out

a happy sigh. POOF!

Just then Mr. Crocker appeared.

"Timmy Turner, you ruined
school property and
disrupted classes.
You are worse than Francis!"
"Timmy—worse than me?"
Francis shook as he walked by.
"Now that's scary!"